A present for

_____

with love from

_____

to mark the giant leap of the moon landings
on July 20th 1969

Jo Earlam

Archie SPACE DOG!

Written by Jo Earlam
Illustrations by Mark Hannon

Published by Turtletastic Titles

The puppy was born in the wild, a homeless, unwanted stray ..... a small terrier with a giant dream - and the moon to light his way.

Rabbit?! Archie's ears pricked up, his nose twitched, sniff-sniff. Squirrel?! Sniff-sniff-sniff.

Archie buried his nose in the long grass and pushed forward into the hedge.

The smell was different and exciting.

Perhaps, it was of rabbit AND squirrel!
Sniff again.

But when was it left here?

Earlier today? Yesterday? Or longer ago?

More digging was required.

As Archie's nose twitched rapidly, his attention was interrupted by a voice loudly calling:

"Earth to Archie, come in please!

...EARTH TO ARCHIE...

Archie heard,
but took
no notice.

This was his owner Sally.
She often said that to try and get him to walk faster.

And she had silly names for him,
baby names that
were embarrassing –
like now...

"Come on,
Mister Poopy Pants,"
she called out.

"What's taking so long?"

Archie flattened his ears.

Mister Poopy Pants!

That was the most annoying
name Sally called him.

Archie ignored her
and focused instead on the
strong inviting smell,
growling to himself:

"I'm not Mister Poopy Pants. I'm Archie."
But Archie who? Archie what?

As a little dog, with short legs, teeth that stuck out and a coat with long wispy curls, Archie was often teased by bigger dogs.

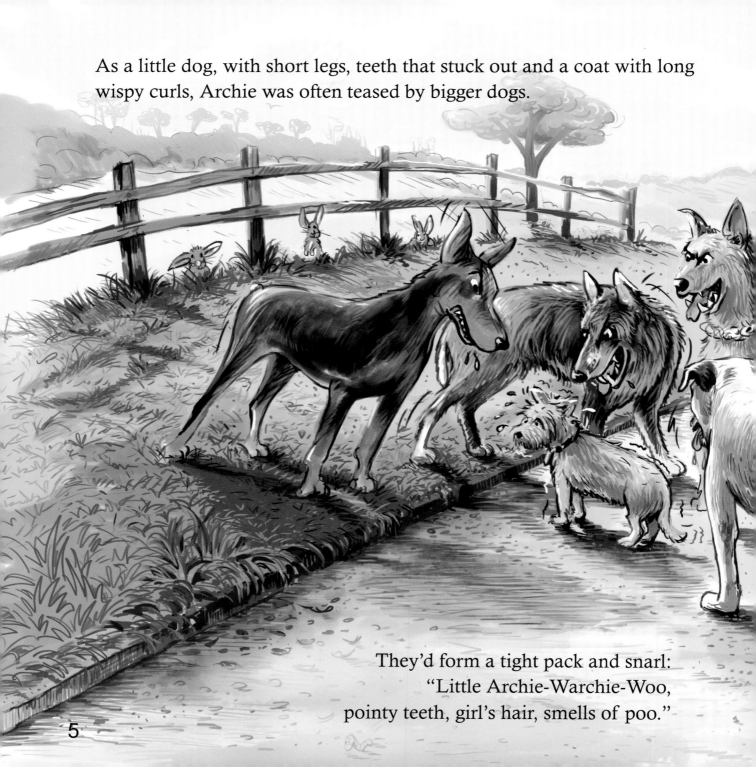

They'd form a tight pack and snarl:
"Little Archie-Warchie-Woo,
pointy teeth, girl's hair, smells of poo."

And it wasn't just dogs that were rude.

Another walker said to Sally that day: "What an odd shape. What type is he?"

"I'm not sure," Sally replied. "He's from a rescue centre."

"Strange mix," chuckled the woman. "Bit of a hairy monster really!"

A hairy monster?!
Mister Poopy Pants!

This was no laughing matter.
Archie was tired of being teased in such a rude way.

"I know. I'll do something amazing," he thought.

Something that would impress everyone... something out of this world.

8

Archie's main walk was
just before the lunchtime news.

Sally would put on the television
and he'd jump on to the back of her chair,
his favourite place to lie.
From here he could watch moving pictures on the large screen.

He'd often nod off listening to endless chatter.
Today's big story was about the first man on the moon,
the anniversary of the moon landings.

It was an incredible moment in history, said a voice.
One small step, but a giant leap.

Archie yawned, his eyes closed, the last words he heard were:
"Earth to…"

"Earth to Archie! Earth to Archie!"

Suddenly his ears pricked up, listening.

This wasn't Sally speaking. This was a man's voice, loud and firm, but with an echo, as if coming from far away.

"Earth to Archie! Come in Space Dog."

Space Dog!

WOW. That's me, thought Archie.

Still drowsy and half asleep, his nose began to twitch. He could smell something. What was it?

Opening his eyes, he stepped forward for a closer sniff.

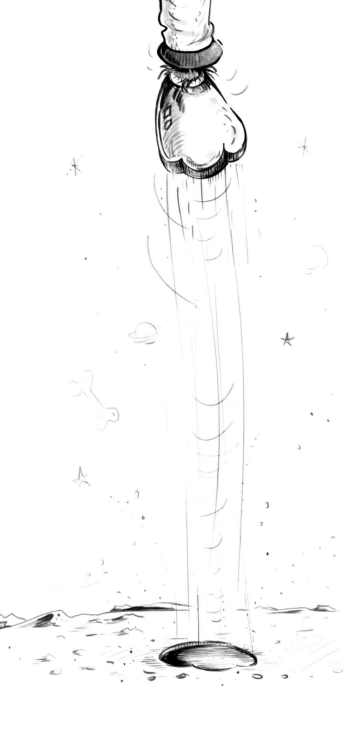

"Whoa!"

As he put down one small
paw, his whole body was
lifted as if in a giant leap.

A giant leap, thought Archie,
like on the moon.

Somewhere you got to
in a space ship,
wearing a space suit.

Archie stood tall on his back legs

and looked down

at his body.

He was no hairy monster, he was wearing a smart silver suit and had a glass-fronted helmet on his head.

As he looked about, there were no flowers, no trees,
just a grey stony surface.

It was nothing like he'd seen before, but with a very familiar
strong smell.

Archie knew it in an instant.

Rabbits!

Eyes wide open and all senses alert,
he saw white tails in the distance...
the fantastic white tails of brightly
coloured giant bunnies bounding
along with giant steps.

Archie took off across the
moon's bumpy lunar landscape.

17

18

He felt
amazing.

19

One
small dog
chasing
giant
leaping
rabbits...

20

"Wake-up!" A voice spoke loudly in his ear.

Still trembling, Archie slowly raised an eyelid,
and saw he was on the back of the chair.

Sally was standing beside him.
"You looked as if you were trying to catch
rabbits on the moon," she said.

"You were miles away dreaming,
Mister Poopy Pants."

But Archie knew this was more than a dream.

It had been real and out of this world.

And it meant he would no longer worry about being called names or laughed at again.

He closed his eyes, and said, with a contented sigh: "I'm not Mister Poopy Pants. I'm Archie, Space Dog!"

24

For we all like to dream -
even tiny terriers with a funny face
can do something amazing,
to find a happy space.

In tribute to the many small dogs who were sent into space, so that mankind could achieve a giant leap of walking on the moon.

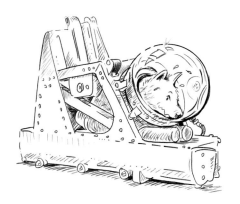

Throughout the 1950s and 60s, the Soviet Union used dogs more than 50 times to see if sending humans into space was possible. They wore pressure suits and acrylic glass bubble helmets and were mostly strays. Many of the dogs survived including Strelka, who went on to have six puppies after her orbital flight in 1960.
The first dog sent on an orbital flight was Laika aboard Sputnik 2, on November 3rd, 1957.

Archie was born on November 3rd, 2004. He was part of a litter of pups whose mother was a stray. All were taken in by a rescue centre. Archie was given a home by author Jo Earlam, who does say: "Earth to Archie…" and call him 'Mister Poopy Pants', knowing that really he is 'Archie, Space Dog'.

In some folklore there is said to be a rabbit that lives on the moon, based on markings on its surface.

RABBIT DISCLAIMER: Archie has never caught a rabbit, and hopes no rabbits are upset by his story.